Dangerous Journey

WILLIAM B. EERDMANS PUBLISHING COMPANY

GRAND RAPIDS, MICHIGAN

Worldwide coedition organized and produced by
Lion Hudson plc, Mayfield House,
256 Banbury Road, Oxford OX2 7DH
Tel: +44 (0) 1865 302750 Fax: +44 (0) 1865 302757
Email: coed@lionhudson.com
www.lionhudson.com

This edition published in the USA by
Wm B Eerdmans Publishing Co.
2140 Oak Industrial Drive, NE
Grand Rapids, Michigan 49505
Manufactured at KWF Printing Pte Ltd, Singapore, in August 2013, 19th printing

13 14 15 16   21 20 19

Library of Congress Cataloging-in-Publication data
A catalog record of this book is available from
the Library of Congress.

ISBN 978-0-8028-3619-9

This arrangement of *Pilgrim's Progress*
made by Oliver Hunkin
Designed by Three's Company
5 Dryden Street, London WC2E 9NW

Yorkshire Television would like to thank
the Dulverton Trust and the S.P.C.K. for
helping to make this project possible.

Contents

Introduction

In the year 1676, a poor tinker named John Bunyan was imprisoned in Bedford Gaol. While he was there, he began to write one of the most famous books in the English language. Pictures came crowding through his mind – faster than he could put them into words: quagmires and steep hills; sunny valleys and dark glens; a gloomy castle – its courtyard strewn with bones; a market town with all the bustle of a fair; and a narrow road – from which one must not stray – running uphill and down dale to the Dark River and the Shining Gate.

Bunyan was forty-seven when he wrote the *Pilgrim's Progress*, and he drew on two main sources: first, his knowledge of the Bible; secondly, his considerable knowledge of the world. Thus he had in mind the escape of Lot from Sodom, as he wrote of the escape of Christian from the City of Destruction. There were many Pliables in his own congregation. Mr Greatheart was a veteran of Cromwell's army. As to Vanity Fair, it was probably modelled on Stourbridge Fair, near Cambridge; and the trial of Faithful before Lord Hate-good was based on Bunyan's own treatment at the hands of Justice Keeling.

Bunyan tells his story as if it happened in a dream. He had no one to help him. He showed his work to no one, till it was complete. Then many of his pious friends were shocked. It was, they said, an idle tale about giants, and lions, and goblins, and warriors sometimes fighting with monsters, and sometimes being lightly entertained by ladies in their palaces.

To start with, it is true, the *Pilgrim's Progress* seems to have been published chiefly for the cottage and the servants' hall. The paper, the printing and the engravings were all of the meanest description. But rapidly the fame of Bunyan grew, and his work has become recognized by millions of readers not as an idle tale at all, but as a story with a hidden meaning – an 'allegory' of that Dangerous Journey, which is, in fact, the journey of Everyman from this world to the next.

Oliver Hunkin

I

The Slough of Despond

As I walked through the wilderness of this world, I lighted on a certain place and laid me down to sleep; and as I slept, I dreamed a dream.

I dreamed that I saw a man, with his face turned away from his own house — a book in his hand, and a great burden on his back. I looked and saw him open the book and read therein; and, as he read, he wept and trembled; and not being able to contain himself, he broke out with a lamentable cry, saying:

What shall I do to be saved?

For he lived in the City of Destruction, which he learnt from his book was doomed to be burned with fire from heaven, in which fearful overthrow both himself, and his wife and their four sons would miserably perish — unless some way of escape could be found.

So Christian (for that was his name) went home to talk to his family. And they were greatly worried, not because they believed that what he said was true, but because they thought some kind of madness had got into the poor man. And as it was drawing towards night, they hoped that sleep might settle his brains. With all haste they put him to bed.

But the night was as troublesome to him as the day; wherefore, instead of sleeping, he spent it in sighs and tears. So, when morning was come, and they asked him how he was, he told them:

Worse! Worse!

He also started talking to them again, but they began to lose patience. Sometimes they would deride him: sometimes they would chide him; and sometimes they would quite neglect him.

So Christian went by himself into the fields — still reading his book and carrying his burden, and greatly distressed in his mind. He looked this way and that way, as if he would run, yet he stood still, because he couldn't tell which way to go.

Then — in the distance — he saw a man approaching. His name was Evangelist, and he asked Christian:

What are you weeping for?
Sir, he answered, *this book in my hand tells me to flee from the wrath to come. Also, I fear that this burden, which is upon my back, will sink me lower than the grave. Therefore, I need to get rid of it.*
If this is so, said Evangelist, *then why are you standing still?*
Because I don't know where to go, he answered.
Then Evangelist pointed with his finger over a wide field.
Do you see yonder wicket-gate, he asked.
No, said Christian.
Then do you see a shining light?
I think I do, said Christian.
Then said Evangelist:
Keep that light in your eye, and go in that direction. So shall you reach the gate. There, when you knock, it will be told you what to do.

So I saw in my dream that the man began to run. But he hadn't run far, before his wife and children saw him running, and called after him to return. But the man put his fingers in his ears and ran on. He didn't look back, but ran towards the middle of the plain.

The neighbours too came out to see him run, and as he ran, some mocked and others threatened. A couple of them were resolved to fetch him back by force; the name of the one was Obstinate, and the name of the other was Pliable. Now by this time the man had gone a good distance from them. Nevertheless, they pursued after him and overtook him.

Neighbours, why have you come? asked Christian.

To persuade you to come back with us, they said.

That can by no means be, said Christian. *You dwell in the City of Destruction. Be content, good neighbours, to go along with me.*

What! said Obstinate, *and leave our friends and our comforts behind us?*

Yes. For I seek an endless kingdom, which we may inhabit for ever. Read of it, if you will, in my book.

Tush! cried Obstinate. *Away with your book. Will you go back with us or no?*

No, not I.

Pliable so far had held his peace. But now he spoke:

If what Christian says is true, I intend to go with this good man.

Very well, then, replied Obstinate. *I will go back to my own place. I'll be no companion to such fantastical fellows.*

With that, they parted. Obstinate went back and Christian and Pliable went on over the plain, discoursing all the while.

Tell me more, neighbour Christian, enquired Pliable, *about the place to which we're going.*
There are crowns of glory to be given us, and garments shining like the sun, Christian told him.

That's very pleasant; and what else?
There shall be no more crying, said Christian. *For the Owner of the Place will wipe all tears from our eyes.*
Well, my good companion, I'm glad to hear these things. Come on, let's hurry.
I can't go any faster, answered Christian, *with this burden on my back.*

Now I saw in my dream that, as they were hurrying along and talking, they had drawn near to a quagmire in the middle of the plain, which was called the Slough of Despond. And before they knew what was happening, they had both fallen into the bog. It was a bog where many travellers before them had been drowned. Here, therefore, they wallowed, being grievously bedaubed with the dirt. And Christian, because of the burden on his back, began to sink, first knee-deep — then waist-deep — into the loathsome scum.

Neighbour Christian, where are you now? asked Pliable.
Truly, I do not know, Christian replied.
So Pliable began to be offended, and angrily said to his fellow:
Is this the happiness you promised me? If we have such ill speed at our first setting out, what may we expect between this and our journey's end?

With that, having no burden to contend with, Pliable scrambled out — on that side of the Slough which was nearest to his own house. And so he ran off home for a hot bath, leaving Christian to his fate. For his part, Christian was struggling to reach the side of the Slough nearest to the wicket-gate. Which he eventually did, but couldn't clamber out by reason of the burden on his back.

Then I beheld in my dream that a man came to him, whose name was Help, and asked him what he was doing there.

Christian answered: *Sir, I was bidden to go this way by a man called Evangelist.*
But did you not look for the stepping-stones?
Fear followed me so hard, that I fell in, replied Christian.
That is the snare and hazard of this place, said Help. *It so spues out its filth that, at the changes of the weather, these steps are hardly seen. Here, give me your hand.*

So he gave him his hand, and drew him out, and set him on firm ground again. And Christian continued on his way towards the wicket-gate.

Although he didn't know it, worse trouble lay in store. For a certain Mr Worldly Wiseman was now seen crossing the field to meet him. He dwelt in the town of Carnal Policy — a very great town, hard-by where Christian lived. This man then, having some inkling of him — for Christian's departure from the City of Destruction was much noised abroad — began to question him.

How now, good fellow, where are you going with that great burden?

I'm going to yonder wicket-gate.

Have you a wife and children? asked Mr Worldly Wiseman.

Why, yes, replied Christian. *But I am so heavily weighed down, I can't take pleasure in them any more.*

Who counselled you to start upon this dangerous journey?

A man that came to me. His name, as I remember, was Evangelist.

I thought as much, said Worldly Wiseman. *He is for ever leading travellers astray. There's no more difficult road in the world than the one he's directed you to. I see, by the dirt on you, that you've already been in the Slough of Despond. But that Slough is only the beginning of your troubles. In the way you are going you are likely to encounter far worse things than this — lions, dragons, darkness and death. This has been confirmed by many witnesses. So why should a man so carelessly risk his life, by giving heed to a stranger?*

After pausing for breath, Mr Worldly Wiseman proceeded as follows:

Hear me — I am older than you — and I'll give you some advice. In yonder village there dwells a gentleman whose name is Legality, a very judicious man — a man of very good name. He has skill to help men off with their burdens. He has, to my knowledge, cured several who were going out of their wits because of them. His house is not a mile from this place, and if he's not at home himself, his son — who's called Civility — will help you. Moreover, if you wish, there are houses standing empty in the village at reasonable rates. The food is cheap and good, and you can send for your wife and family, and all live happily together.

Christian, we fear, was all too ready to listen to Mr Worldly Wiseman and leave the straight path he was on.

Sir, which is the way to this honest man's house? he enquired.

Do you see yonder high hill? asked Mr Worldly Wiseman.

Yes, very well.

By that hill you must go, and the first house you come to is Mr Legality's.

Thus did Mr Worldly Wiseman courteously direct poor Christian down the wrong road. For what he had failed to tell him was the hill ahead was a fearsome mountain. It seemed to overhang the road so much that Christian — looking up as the clouds scudded over it — was afraid that it would fall upon his head. Worse than that, there were flashes of fire coming out of it. And Christian, because of his burden, might easily have fallen, and thus early on his journey have been burnt to death. Wherefore, he did sweat and quake for fear.

At that moment, who should appear but Evangelist, coming to meet him with a severe and dreadful countenance, at the sight of which Christian began to blush with shame.

Aren't you the man I found weeping outside the City of Destruction? questioned Evangelist.

Yes, dear sir, I am the man.

Did not I direct you to the little wicket-gate?

Yes, dear sir, replied Christian.

How is it then that you've so quickly turned aside?

I met, you see, a gentleman; and he persuaded me that I might find in the village before me a man who could take off my burden. He said, moreover, he would show me a better way — not so attended with difficulties as the way, sir, that you set me in.

Then said Evangelist: *Stand still a little.*

So he stood trembling. And Evangelist said: *You have rejected the Word of God for the advice of Mr Worldly Wiseman. But Mr Legality cannot free you of your burden. Mr Legality is a cheat. As for his son, Civility, notwithstanding his simpering looks, he cannot help you either.*

As he spoke, there was a great clap of thunder. And Christian called himself a thousand fools for listening to Mr Worldly Wiseman.

I am sorry I have hearkened to this man's counsel, he said, turning back with haste.

He spoke to no one on the way, nor, if anybody asked him, would he give them an answer. He went like one that was all the while treading on forbidden ground, and could by no means think himself safe, till he had regained the road he had abandoned.

But would he ever reach it? He wasn't at all sure. *For narrow is the gate.* it says in his book, *and few are they who find it.*

2

The Interpreter's House

I saw then, in my dream, that ahead of Christian, on a grassy bank, lay three men fast asleep, with fetters on their heels. They were called Simple, Sloth and Presumption.

Christian knew that to sleep on this particular road was like sleeping in the rigging of a ship when a storm was brewing.

Wake up! he cried, *and I will help you off with your irons.*

But they only opened one eye at him, and yawned.

I see no danger, said Simple.

I want to go on sleeping, said Sloth.

Every tub must stand on its own bottom, said Presumption.

Then they all three rolled over, and went to sleep again.

So Christian proceeded on his way, troubled to think that men in such danger should so little esteem his kindness in waking them. And we are now to learn how wise it was of Christian to warn them. For as he drew near to the narrow wicket-gate, he saw that it was firmly closed.

And even as he reached it, he felt the wind of an arrow swish past his ear, and bury itself in the woodwork. Looking round in terror, he now saw, on the opposite hill, a strong castle with a host of dark, menacing figures on the battlements.

Christian didn't dally. Over the gate was written: KNOCK, AND IT SHALL BE OPENED UNTO YOU.

He knocked with all his might.

A second arrow narrowly missed him.

Who's there? asked a voice.

A poor burdened traveller. I come from the City of Destruction, and I'm going to the Celestial City.

To his relief, the gate was quickly opened, and a hand pulled him in.

Then Christian asked the Guardian of the Gate, whose name was Goodwill:

What mean these arrows?

To which he answered:

Yonder castle belongs to Beelzebub, the Prince of the Devils. Both he and his soldiers will shoot their darts at anyone who tries to enter here. They aim to kill you before you can reach safety. You are fortunate to be alive.

I tremble and rejoice, said Christian,

Why do you come alone? asked Goodwill.

Because none of my neighbours and none whom I encountered on the road saw the danger.

Did none of them follow you?

Pliable came with me a little way, until we fell — both together — into the Slough of Despond, Christian answered. *At that he was discouraged, and would not adventure further.*

Alas, poor man! Is it not worth running a few risks, when the Heavenly City is your destination? Goodwill asked.

But I'm not one to talk, replied Christian. *I also nearly turned aside, persuaded by the arguments of Mr Worldly Wiseman. And I don't know what would have become of me, had not Evangelist met me again, when I was musing in the midst of my dumps. And truth to tell, I'm still much inconvenienced by this burden that is upon my back.*

Then I saw in my dream that Christian asked him if he could not help him off with his burden.

However hard I try, said Christian, *I don't seem able to move it.*

No man can get it off you, said Goodwill. *But keep to the straight and narrow path, and it will lead you to the Place of Deliverance.*

So Christian began to gird his loins, and to address himself to his journey.

How far will it be? he asked himself, as he plodded on his way.

His next stop was the House of the Interpreter, who, Goodwill had told him, could give him useful lessons for his journey. It was a large and mysterious house, such as one visits in dreams. Its Master, in answer to his knock, asked him what he wanted.

Sir, said Christian, *I am a man that is going to Mount Zion. And I was told that, if I called here, you would show me excellent things, which would help me.*

Come in, said the Interpreter.

First he led him into a parlour, which was full of dust, because it was never swept. So the Interpreter called for a serving-maid to sweep it. But the dust began to fly, and Christian began to choke. Never had there been such dust. He groped around blindly. Then he heard the Interpreter tell the maid:

Bring hither water, and sprinkle the room.

All at once the dust had cleared, and the maid was sweeping it up with pleasure.

This parlour, said the Interpreter, *is the soul of man clogged with the dust of sin. But see how easily, by God's grace, it can be cleansed.*

I saw, in my dream, that the Interpreter took Christian by the hand again, and led him into a very dark room, where there sat a man in an iron cage. Now the man seemed very sad. He sat with his eyes looking down to the ground, and his hands folded together, and he sighed as if his heart would break.

Then said Christian:

Who is this?

Talk with him and see, said the Interpreter.

What used you to be? asked Christian.

I was once a flourishing professor, both in my own eyes, and also in the eyes of others, answered the man. *I was on my way, as I thought, to the Celestial City, and I was confident that I would get there.*

But what did you do to bring yourself to this condition? Christian asked.

I failed to keep watch, the man replied. *I followed the pleasures of this world, which promised me all manner of delights. But they proved to be an empty bubble. And now I am shut up in this iron cage — a man of despair, who can't get out.*

No further explanations were given. No one said who put him there. But the Interpreter whispered to Christian:

Bear well in mind what you have seen.

Finally, Christian was led to a gateway like the one which he had lately entered. Beside it sat a man at a table, with a book and inkhorn before him to take the name of anyone who wished to pass through. But the gate was guarded by fierce men in armour, ready to do what hurt and mischief they could to any traveller. And though there stood a great company of people desirous of going in, they didn't dare. Then, as it were a scene upon the stage, Christian saw a valiant man approach.

Set down my name, sir, he said.

That done, he drew his sword and rushed upon the armed men, who laid upon him with deadly force. But the man, not at all discouraged, fell to cutting and hacking most resolutely. So, after he had received and given many wounds, he cut his way to safety.

I think I know the lesson of this, said Christian triumphantly, as he resumed his journey. *My safety will depend, it seems, not on cleverness, but on simple courage.*

How his burden had got on his back in the first place, and why nobody else had burdens—as happens in dreams—we are not told. But never had he been so eager as he was now to be rid of it. And that—did he but know it—was half the battle.

Now I saw in my dream that the road, from then on, was fenced on either side with a wall. The wall was named Salvation. Along this road did burdened Christian run. Or should we say, he did his best to run, so far as he could, with that load upon his back.

At the foot of a hill, he passed an open tomb. Then up again, upon a little knoll, he found himself beneath a wayside cross. And as its shadow fell across him, so suddenly the burden, slipping from his shoulders, fell from off his back. It tumbled down the hill. It tumbled into the mouth of the tomb. It was never seen again.

Christian kept feeling behind his back. He couldn't believe it. For it was very surprising to him that the simple act of gazing at the cross had set him free, and his burden of guilt was gone.

As he stood there in amazement, behold three Shining Ones appeared. The first one said:
Your soul is now swept clean of sin.
The second stripped him of his mud-stained rags, and gave him bright new clothes. The third one handed him a parchment.

Guard it carefully, he said, *and surrender it only when you have reached the gate of the Celestial City.*

Great dangers lay ahead of him But for the moment he was light as air. So Christian gave three leaps for joy, and went on singing.

Who would true valour see
Let him come hither;
One here will constant be
Come wind, come weather;
There's no discouragement
Shall make him once relent
His first avowed intent
To be a pilgrim.

The Hill Difficulty

As Christian now set off again – free of his burden and light of foot – suddenly, to the left of him, two strangers jumped over the wall, and came at him apace. The name of the one was Formalist and the name of the other Hypocrisy.

Gentlemen, asked Christian. *Where have you come from, and where are you going?*

We were born in the land of Vain-glory, and we are on our way to the Heavenly City, they replied.

Then why did you jump over the wall, instead of coming through the narrow wicket-gate? Did you not know that he who climbs in by some other way is a thief and a robber?

It's a long way round to the wicket-gate, answered Formalist and Hypocrisy. *Our countrymen always take this short-cut. They've been doing it for hundreds of years, so it can't be wrong.*

But it's breaking the rules of the journey.

What's it matter how *we did it,* said the two men. *If we are in, we are in.*

I walk by the rule of my Master; you follow your own fancies, Christian answered.

To this they gave him no answer, only they looked upon each other and laughed. So they continued on their way, the three of them together. I beheld then that they reached a cross roads. One broad road turned to the left; another broad road

turned to the right; while the narrow road went straight on – up the great black back of the Hill called Difficulty.

Which one would they choose? Formalist chose to go to the left, which led him into a dark wood. Did he but know it, the road was called Danger, and he lost his way for ever. Hypocrisy chose to go to the right, which led him into rough ground, full of holes and hummocks. Did he but know it, the road was called Destruction. Here he stumbled and fell, and rose no more. As for Christian, he paused and drank at a spring to refresh himself. Then after looking both ways, he started briskly *straight on* up the hill.

But soon he was wondering—had he chosen wisely? For he went from running to walking, from walking to clambering; and now he was on his hands and knees, because of the steepness of the place. Then, just as he was about to give up, midway to the top of the hill, he espied a pleasant arbour, made by the Lord of the hill, for the refreshing of weary travellers.

Here Christian gratefully sat down to rest; and pulling out the parchment, which the Shining One had given him, he read it to his comfort. He also looked with admiration at the embroidered coat, which had been given him as he stood by the cross. Thus pleasing himself awhile, in the drowsy warmth of the afternoon sun, he first fell into a slumber, and then into a fast sleep.

When he awoke it was late evening. So he quickly
rose up, and hastened on his way. Then, coming
towards him, he heard the sound of running feet, and
out of the twilight, two men appeared. The name of
the one was Timorous, and of the other, Mistrust.

Sirs, what's the matter? asked Christian *You run
the wrong way.*

*It's true we were going to the Heavenly City, and
had climbed the Hill Difficulty,* said Timorous.
*But the further we went the more danger we
met. Therefore we turned, and are going back.
There were these two lions in the way,* added
Mistrust. *Whether asleep or awake we knew not.
But we agreed that, if we came within reach,
they could tear us to pieces.*

So saying, Timorous and Mistrust ran on down the
hill, leaving Christian much perplexed. For he now
said to himself:

If I go forward, I shall perish. Likewise, if I go back to my own country, I shall perish. What am I to do?

Then he remembered his parchment, and felt for it under his coat. It had always been a help and comfort to him. But though he felt everywhere, he couldn't find it. He must have dropped it. And it should have been his passport, without which he couldn't enter the Celestial City. As so often happens in dreams, that which he dreaded most had come to pass. He had no choice; he must go back.

So, sighing deeply, and chiding himself for being such a fool, he retraced his steps, looking on this side and that. It was growing darker all the time, and the night was full of whispers and unearthly sounds. Dark though it was when he reached the arbour, God directed his eye to the place where the parchment lay. It must have slipped from him, while he was asleep. With great joy, he picked it up. But then he cried:

Oh dear! I have trod the same road three times, which I should have trod but once! How far might I have been by now upon my way.

He truly feared that he would be benighted.

O thou sinful sleep! He cried, *For thy sake, I must walk without the sun.*

He also remembered how Mistrust and Timorous had been frightened by the lions.

These beasts, he said to himself, *seek their prey by night, and if they should meet me in the dark, how should I escape them?*

And again he asked himself:

What shall I do?

There was still light enough to read his parchment, and this is what he read:

Desire now a better country – that is, the Heavenly One.

And with these words to strengthen him, Christian resumed his climb. Lifting up his eyes, he saw against the sky the towers of a stately Palace – the Palace Beautiful.

Here perhaps, he thought, *they'll give me lodgings for the night.*

So I saw in my dream that he made greater haste. But as he drew nearer, he could hear in the darkness the roaring of the lions. The only way forward was along a narrow passage, which was about a furlong from the porter's lodge. This, he knew, was the place from which Mistrust and Timorous had fled. And Christian was never so near to running back after them

But the porter at the lodge, whose name was Watchful, perceiving now that Christian made a halt, cried out:

Is your strength so small? Fear not the lions. They are on long chains. If you keep strictly to the beam of light, in the centre of the path, they cannot reach you.

So Christian moved on. He took good heed to the directions of the porter. At the same time, he trembled for fear of the lions, for now they were on either side of him, straining at their chains.

And how they roared, and snapped at him!

And how they tried to catch him by the foot!

But Christian soldiered on boldly. And in another minute he was through and had reached the gate unharmed. Then, somewhat breathlessly, he asked the porter:

Sir may I lodge here for the night?

That depends, he said, looking at him suspiciously. *What's your name? And what is your business?*

My name is Christian. I am come from the City of Destruction, and am going to the Heavenly City.

But how does it happen that you come so late? asked the porter. *The sun is set.*

I had been here sooner, but — wretched man that I am — I slept in the arbour that stands on the hillside, Christian explained.

And there I dropped my parchment, and came without it to the brow of the hill. Then, feeling for it, and finding it not, I was forced to go back for it.

Well, that's a sorry tale, to be sure, said the porter. *But I will summon one of the young ladies that live here. If she likes your talk, she may bring you in to the rest of the family — or contrariwise she may not!*

So Watchful, the porter, rang the bell, and there appeared at the sound of it a grave and beautiful damsel, called Discretion.

She questioned him closely, asking him what he had seen and met with in the way; and he told her. So she smiled, but the tears stood in her eyes. And after a little pause, she said, to his relief:

We have to be careful whom we admit here. But this house was built by the Lord of the hill for the benefit of pilgrims. So, with the Lord's blessing, come in.

Then he bowed his head and followed her into the house. And when she and her sisters had made ready, they sat down to meat. After supper, they committed themselves to their Lord for protection, and then betook themselves to rest. Christian they laid in a large upper chamber, whose windows opened towards the sun-rising. And the name of chamber was Peace.

So, for a little while, Christian was safe. And much he needed to renew his strength, for on the morrow — though he knew it not — he had to fight the Foul Fiend, Apollyon.

The Fight with Apollyon

Then I saw in my dream that on the morrow Christian desired to go forward on his journey. But the ladies of the house, whose names were Charity, Piety, Prudence and Discretion, told him that he should not depart thence, till they had shown him the rarities of the place.

For if the day be clear, they said, *we will show you the Delectable Mountains.*

So he consented, and stayed. And when morning was up, they took him to the roof of the Palace.

Look to the south, they said.

So he did. And behold, the mountains in the sunlight were indeed delectable, and beautified with woods.

From the top of these mountains, they told him, *you may see the gate of the Celestial City.*

This greatly encouraged him. Yet in truth, the City was still a long way off, and the journey, as we know, had all to be done on foot. So once again Christian desired to be going. But once again they detained him. Now it was the turn of Charity to question him.

Have you a family? asked Charity. *Are you a married man?*

I have a wife and four small children, Christian replied.

Then why didn't you bring them along with you, to share in your felicity? she questioned.

At this, our traveller began to weep:

Oh, how willingly I would have done so. But they were all of them averse to going on pilgrimage. My wife was afraid of losing the comforts of this world; and my children were given to the foolish delights of youth. So, what with one thing and another, to my great grief, they would not come.

From all that had befallen him so far you may think he did prudently to make the journey first alone. The other damsels said as much.

But still they would not let him go, till they had led him to the Armoury. Here they showed him some of the objects with which the servants of the Lord had done wonderful things. They showed him Moses' rod; the hammer and nail with which Jael slew Sisera; the pitchers, trumpets, and lamps too, with which Gideon put to flight the armies of Midian. They showed him also the jawbone of the ass, with which Samson did such mighty deeds, and they showed him the sling and the stone, with which David slew Goliath.

Then they fitted Christian out with the armour, which their Lord provided for the use of travellers, that they should be ready for any assaults along the way, and that they should stand their ground, when things were at their worst, and *having done all to stand.* First, the helmet and breastplate, that could save his life. Then the faithful shield, to fend off the fiery darts of the wicked. Then the trusty sword, that could cut through anything. Finally his feet were shod with shoes that would never wear out. For he was setting out, they said, not against human foes, but against the wiles of the Devil.

Thus fully armed did Christian hurry to the gate, and there he asked the porter:

Have you seen any other pilgrim pass this way?

The porter answered: *Yes.*

Pray, did you know him? asked Christian.

I asked him his name, and he told me it was Faithful.

He is my townsman, my near neighbour, Christian exclaimed. *He comes from the place where I was born. How far do you think he is ahead of me?*

By this time he will be below the hill, answered the porter

Well, good porter, the Lord be with you. If I hasten, I may catch him up.

He was not to overtake his friend that day. Instead, he found himself in a solitary valley, called the Valley of Humiliation. Here, afer he had stopped to partake of the bread and wine and raisins, which the damsels had given him, he was feeling well content.

Perhaps, he said to himself, *the worst is over.*

All of a sudden, a darkness fell across the sun. What could it be? He roused himself, and there he saw, stalking towards him, the towering shape of a Foul Fiend. He was at least nine feet high, and the nearer he came, the more hideous he grew. He had scales like a fish, and they are his pride. He had wings like a dragon, and feet like a bear, and out of his belly came fire and smoke.

As happens in a dream, Christian recognized the Fiend at once, and knew his name. It was Apollyon. Terrified, he cast in his mind whether to go back, or to stay firm. Then, considering that he had no armour on his back, and to turn his back to the monster would give him the advantage, he resolved to stay firm.

The Fiend had now drawn very close. He looked upon Christian with a disdainful countenance, and thus began to question him:

Where have you come from?

I've come from the City of Destruction, which is the place of all evil.

By this I perceive that you are one of my subjects, said Apollyon. *For I am the Prince of that city, and all that country is mine. Why then are you running away from your Prince?*

I was indeed born in your dominions, admitted Christian. *But I have given my allegiance to another, who is the King of Princes. How can I now, with fairness, go back on this?*

You did the same to me, and yet I am willing to pass it over, replied Apollyon. *What I promised you was in my infancy,* said Christian. *Besides, to tell you the truth, I like his service better than yours.*

You have already been unfaithful to him, exclaimed Apollyon. *You fell in the Slough of Despond. You slept, and let fall your parchment. And in all you say and do, you are inwardly desirous of vain-glory.*

Too well I know it. Yet the King whom I serve is merciful and ready to forgive.

I am the enemy of this King, said Apollyon. *I hate his person, his laws and his people. Moreover, there is no prince who will lightly lose his subjects, neither will I lose you. Give him the slip, and work for me, and your wages shall be doubled.*

I know your wages, you destroying Apollyon. They are not such as a man can live on. They are the wages of death.

Then Apollyon broke into a grievous rage:

What you say is true. Therefore prepare yourself to die!

Apollyon, beware what you're doing, cried Christian. *For I am on the King's Highway — the way of Holiness. Therefore take heed of yourself.*

But Apollyon straddled over the whole breadth of the way, and barred his path:

I am void of fear in this matter. I swear by my Infernal Den that you shall go no further. Here will I spill your soul!

Without more ado, the Fiend threw a flaming dart at Christian's breast. But Christian had his shield in his hand, and so prevented him. Then Christian drew his sword, for he saw it was time to bestir himself. And the Fiend made fast at him, and threw his darts as thick as hail. And though he did all he could to avoid them, and in spite of the new armour that he wore, Christian was wounded in the head, the hand, the foot, and forced to yield ground.

But he still resisted as manfully as he could hoping perhaps some other traveller would hear the clash of arms and come to his assistance. But any within earshot were too cowardly to fight; they made a wide detour rather than encounter such a fiend.

The combat now had lasted half the day. You couldn't imagine, if you had not been there, what yelling and roaring Apollyon made, and what sighs and groans burst from the Pilgrim's heart. For you must know that, by reason of his wounds, Christian was growing weaker by the hour. Then Apollyon saw his chance, and came in close, and, wrestling with Christian, gave him such a dreadful fall, that his sword flew from his hand.

Now I am sure of you! the Fiend cried. And kneeling on him, as he lay helplessly upon his back, he pressed him near to death. But as God would have it, while Apollyon was preparing his final blow, thereby to make an end of this good man, Christian nimbly stretched out his hand for his sword, and caught it, saying:

Rejoice not against me, O mine enemy; when I fall, I shall arise.

With that, he ran Apollyon through. And with a terrible roar — as one that had received a mortal wound — the Fiend drew back.

Then for the first time Christian smiled. For, looking up, he saw Apollyon spread his dragon's wings, and fly away, dripping blood over the fields as he went. So the battle was over, and Christian offered thanks for his deliverance. But he, too, was bleeding copiously and if he was to bleed to death, his victory would have been in vain.

Then in his mercy God directed him towards a certain tree, the Tree of Life, the leaves of which he now applied to all his wounds. They staunched the flow of blood, and he was healed immediately. He also sat down in that place to eat and drink, and so refreshed, Christian went forward to the Valley's end. He left his heavy armour there, but kept his sword still drawn in his hand.

For all I know, he said, *some other enemy lies even now in wait for me.*

Indeed, far worse things lay ahead of him, worse even than his combat with the Fiend.

The Valley of the Shadow of Death

I saw in my dream that Christian had now to enter another Valley — the darkest he had yet encountered. It was a very lonely place, where there was no water. No one lived there, and its silence was the silence of the grave. Here Christian was to be more sternly tested than ever in his fight with Apollyon.

It started when two men suddenly ran out from behind some trees, shouting:

Back! Go back!

Why? What's the matter? asked Christian.

Matter! We were going the way you're going, and went as far as we dare.

But what have you met with? queried Christian.

Why, the Valley itself, said the men. *It's as black as pitch down there. The only sound is the howling of the Damned who, having entered there, have never been able to find their way out. In a word, it is every whit dreadful, and utterly without order. For we'd have you know, this is none other than the Valley of the Shadow of Death.*

But there is no other way to the Celestial City, Christian declared.

Be that as it may, it's not the way we're going, said the two men.

And they ran on past Christian, waving their arms in terror.

Christian, notwithstanding, went forward sword in hand, feeling his way step by step. For the path was exceedingly narrow. On the right, there lay a very deep ditch, into which many had fallen in all ages, and perished miserably. On the left there lay a marsh so dangerous that even a good man, if he were sucked in, was never seen again; for he could find no bottom for his foot to stand on. It was all so dark that, when Christian tried to avoid the marsh, he almost fell headlong into the ditch. He never knew whether his next step might not be his last.

Then he saw ahead of him the light of a fire burning. For a moment, as one does in dreams, he again thought the worst was over.

Some light to see by! This is better!

But he was utterly mistaken. For what he had seen was the very mouth of Hell itself, out of which were belching clouds of evil-smelling smoke, which added to the darkness all around; and the air was full of doleful voices, and the rush of wings. Apparitions against which his trusty sword, with which he had put Apollyon to flight, was of no avail, for they cared not for his sword. Sometimes they brushed against him with such a force that he feared they would push him off the path, and he would drop into the depths of Hell, and be lost for ever.

These rushings to and fro were heard by him for several miles together, till he could go no further, and dearly wanted to go back. But then he thought:

By now I may be half-way through the Valley. And the danger of going back may be as great as the danger of going forward.

So he resolved to go on, and he shouted into the darkness with a vehement voice:

I will walk in the strength of the Lord God!

And for a while, silence fell about him once again.

But not for long. For now one of the wicked ones came up behind him, and started whispering many base suggestions in his ear, which he verily thought proceeded from his own mind. And this worried poor Christian more than anything he had met with before; he might easily have fallen on his sword, and put an end to his misery.

At that moment, he thought he heard the voice of a man going before him, saying:

Though I walk through the Valley of the Shadow of Death, I will fear no evil, for thou art with me.

Immediately Christian took courage, and that for three reasons:

1 He gathered from this that there were in the Valley others who feared God, beside himself.

2 He perceived that God was with THEM; and if with them, why not with HIM?

3 He hoped to overtake them, and have their company.

Moreover, day was dawning, and he could look back. And by the light of day, he saw those hobgoblins and dragons of the Pit, which had brushed against him in the dark, but all afar off, for, after daybreak, they dare not come near. Then said Christian, quoting from Scripture:

He has turned the shadow of death into the morning.

The sunrise brought another benefit for Christian. For, though the first part of the Valley was dangerous enough, the second part was, if possible, even more so. From the hillock where he stood, he could see the path ahead, that it was cunningly set with pitfalls, traps and secret nets, so that, had it been dark, he couldn't have escaped death, even if he'd had a thousand lives. As it was, he once became entangled in a net, and only his trusty sword could free him. And twice a man-trap, snapping shut beneath him, almost caught his leg. And time and time again he nearly fell to his destruction, as the ground crumbled under him.

Then I saw in my dream, just when he believed he was out of the Valley, he came across a grisly sight indeed: a pile of skulls and mangled bones, lying outside a cave – all that remained of pilgrims who had gone that way before. Even as he stopped to peer within, a sudden hand came out at him. It tried to seize him by the throat; he only just leapt back in time.

It seems that once two giants had lived there, both with a taste for pilgrims' blood. But one had now been dead for many years; the other, whose name was Pagan, though he was still alive, was, by reason of his age, grown too stiff in his joints to venture far. He could now do little more than sit in the cave's mouth, biting his nails in frustration at not being able to molest the pilgrims passing by. So Christian came to no more harm, and hurried on his way.

Then, on the path ahead of him, he saw a man running as if for his life. He recognized him as Faithful, his friend and neighbour – the same whom the porter at the Palace Beautiful had informed him of.

Ho, there! he shouted. *Wait till I catch you up!* But Faithful only ran the faster, crying:

There's an avenger at my heels! I'm running for my life!

(He was half-crazy, still, with fear after passing through the Valley.)

In the end, Christian, summoning all his strength, did outrun Faithful, and was able to reassure him. And soon they were walking most lovingly together, each telling the other his adventures on the way. Faithful, it seemed, had escaped the Slough, but a wench, whose name was Wanton, who was nearly his undoing. Apollyon, however, he didn't have to fight.

How long, dear friend, did you stay in the City of Destruction, before you set off after me? asked Christian.

Till I could stay no longer, replied Faithful. *For there was great talk, after you were gone, that our city would in a short time be burnt to the ground with fire from heaven.*

What! Did your neighbours talk so? asked Christian.

Yes, it was for a while in everyone's mouth.

And did no more of them, except you, come out to escape the danger?

Though there was much talk I don't think they firmly believed it, said Faithful. *For I heard some of them speak deridingly of you and your desperate journey.*

Thus they went on talking, and so made the hours pass easily, which might otherwise have been tedious to them. Then, of a sudden, Faithful spied a man on the road ahead.

Who's that? he cried, once more consumed with fear.

But Christian said: *It's my good friend, Evangelist.*

And so it was. Evangelist had come, as was his wont, to warn them yet again:

Don't think you're out of gun-shot of the Devil. For as the Gospel says, my sons, in order to enter the Kingdom of Heaven, you have to pass through many tribulations.

Then he pointed into the distance.

You will soon come to a town, he said. *You can see it there before you. It is the town of Vanity. And in that town you will have enemies.*

Then he added, looking fixedly upon them both:

Therefore quit yourselves like men, and commit your souls to God, as to a faithful Creator. For one of you will die a painful death.

With that, Evangelist as suddenly departed, and Faithful and Christian were left wondering:

Which of us two did he mean?

There was nothing for it, but to go forward and find out.

Vanity Fair

Then I saw, in my dream, that Christian and Faithful descended into the town of Vanity. They could hear the sounds of a fair, which is held all the year round; it is called Vanity Fair.

Most fairs are merry places. But not this one — not for our travellers. For here one of them was destined to die. As in other fairs of less importance, the streets are named after different countries. There is the French Row and the Italian Row, and the British Row, where the commodities of these countries are sold and bought.

Indeed, there are stalls where every foolish trifle in the world is up for sale. Knick-knacks of gold and silver; baubles, and bric-à-brac and precious stones. In addition, you could buy titles, and honours, and preferments to high office, and vain pleasures and empty delights of every kind. Moving busily among the crowds are cheats, and rogues and mountebanks. The air is full of fearful oaths; and murder, they say, is as common as theft.

This Fair is no newly-erected business, but a thing of long-standing. More than a thousand years ago, there were pilgrims walking to the Celestial City, as these two honest persons are. And Beelzebub, the Prince of the Demons, with Apollyon and Legion and their companions, perceiving that the pilgrims' way lay through this town of Vanity, contrived to set up a Fair here. For he that would by-pass this town, must needs go out of the world!

So Christian and Faithful had to pass through this lusty Fair. And hoping they would go unnoticed, they pulled their collars up around their faces. But the rabble were quick to spot them. First, they jeered at them for their outlandish clothes. Then they jeered at them for their foreign accents. Finally, they asked them angrily:

Why aren't you buying our merchandise? Buy! Buy! Buy!

We buy only the truth, they said, and put their fingers in their ears, and sought to turn away their eyes from beholding vanity. At that, the townsmen were the more enraged, and the noisiest of hubbubs ensued.

News of the hubbub presently reached the Burgomaster. He took the pilgrims to be lunatics, and bade his officers arrest them as disturbers of the peace, and take their weapons from them.

They were placed in a cage, with their feet in
stocks, as a public spectacle. They lay there for some
time and were made the objects of any man's sport.

For their part, they encouraged one another to trust in the Lord, and behaved themselves most wisely — giving the passers-by good words for bad, not railing for railing, but contrariwise blessing. This further enraged the men of the Fair, who now demanded in loud voices that Christian and Faithful should stand trial in the Courts.

So a day was appointed, and they were brought before the Judge. The Judge was Lord Hate-good. And witnesses were called. The first, whose name was Envy, took the oath. Then, pointing his finger at Faithful, he said:

My lord, I have known this man Faithful for a long time … (which was a lie for a start) He is one of the vilest persons in the country.

Superstition was the second witness.

For myself, he said, *I have no great acquaintance with the prisoner. Nor do I desire to know him further. For in my talk with him, he did condemn our laudable Religion as a thing of nought.*

The third witness was a Mr Pickthank.

My lord, he said, *and you gentlemen all, I too have heard this fellow speak things that ought not to be spoke. He spoke contemptuously of our noble Prince Beelzebub, and of his honourable friends, Lord Luxury, Lord Lechery and Sir Havit Greedy. He also railed at you, my lord who are appointed his Judge. He called you, I regret to say, 'an ungodly villain'.*

It was clear by now that Faithful had been singled out by all three witnesses for their attack. So the Judge addressed himself to Faithful:

You have heard, sirrah, he said coldly, *how these honest gentlemen have witnessed against you. You are, beyond doubt, a vile runagate. Yet, in order that all men may see our gentleness towards you, let us hear what you have to say in your defence.*

I say then, said Faithful, *that in my belief, your Laws and your Religion are flat against the Word of God, and diametrically opposite to Christianity. If you can prove me wrong, then I am ready to recant. As to Mr Pickthank's allegations, I abide by what I said. Your Prince and his attendants — by this gentleman named — are fitter to be in Hell than in this town. And so the Lord have mercy on my soul!*

The Judge, in summing up, quoted many learned instances from the Laws of the Medes and Persians — to prove we know not what. Then he called on the Jury, all lawful men and true, to consider their verdict.

The foreman, Mr Blindman, said:

> *I clearly see this man to be a heretic.*
> *Away with such a fellow,* said Mr No-good.
> *Ay,* said Mr Malice, *for I hate the very looks of him.*
> *A sorry scrub,* said Mr High-mind.
> *Hang him! Hang him!* said Mr Heady.
> *Hanging is too good for him,* said Mr Cruelty.

So, they found him guilty, according to their laws. And after endless indignities, they burnt him at the stake. Thus Faithful met his end.

But I saw in my dream that, behind the crowds, there stood a chariot and horses waiting for Faithful, who (as soon as his enemies had done with him) was taken up into it, and wafted through the clouds to the sound of trumpets. So, in truth, he fared better than his friend, Christian. He would arrive first at the Celestial City, and, having been Faithful unto death, the King would give him a crown of life.

Where had Christian been all this time? Well one of the men of the Fair, whose name was Hopeful, was much moved by the calm deportment of the pilgrims. And, while the people crowded round to see the execution, he succeeded — as sometimes happens in a dream — in spiriting Christian away to safety. And now Christian and Hopeful travelled on together.

Their way took them near the City of Fair Speech.
Four of its untrustworthy citizens came out to salute
them, bowing very low.

We too are going to the Celestial City, they said.
We shall be glad of your company.
Hopeful was for joining them. But Christian had
heard of their city — that it was a place where Money
ruled, and where Religion went in silver slippers. He
also recognized one of them as Mr By-ends, who had
many rich relations; his wife was Lady Feigning's
daughter, and he was a friend to Mr Facing-both-
ways, and to Mr Money-love. So Christian whispered
in Hopeful's ear:
*I like them not as our companions. For they are
very knaves.*

And making their excuses, they hastened on ahead. A little off the road was a hill called Lucre, and from it, a gentleman called Demas shouted out to them:

Ho! Turn aside! There's a silver mine here! With very little trouble, you'll be rich.

Let's go and see, said Hopeful, hopefully.

Not I, said Christian. *I've heard of this place too, that it is dangerous.*

Not dangerous at all, said Demas, though he blushed with shame as he spoke. So Christian hurried Hopeful past.

By now, the citizens of Fair Speech were coming into view. *They* had no hesitation, when Demas beckoned them. *They* were only too pleased to dig for silver.

Lead us to the mine, they said.

But as they looked greedily over the brink, we're told they lost their footing, fell in, and were smothered by the damps that commonly arise. For certain, they were never seen again.

As to Christian, though he had been prudent then, his prudence didn't last. He was soon to make a terrible mistake.

Doubting Castle

It was as well that Christian had Hopeful as his new companion. He would soon be in dire need of him. For I beheld in my dream that they had not journeyed far — the road ahead being very rough, and their feet very tender with travelling — when they became much discouraged.

At this point, Christian espied a stile which led into a meadow, and seemed to be a short-cut.

Here's better going, he said. *Come good Hopeful, let's climb over it.*

What if it leads us out of our way? asked Hopeful.

That's not likely, replied Christian. *Look! There's another man walking ahead of us.*

So over the stile they went, and Christian was well pleased that the path was easier on his feet. But, in leaving the road, he had made a terrible mistake.

For soon night came on, and it grew very dark. They completely lost sight of the pilgrim ahead. (Did they but know it, his name was Vain-confidence.) Suddenly they heard in the darkness a shriek, followed by an eerie silence.

We'll go no further, said Hopeful in a whisper, clutching at Christian's arm.

Who could have thought that this path would lead us nowhere? Christian exclaimed.

I was afraid of it from the first, admitted Hopeful. *I would have spoken up before, only you are older than I.*

Good brother, let's try to go back again, Christian urged him.

But even as they tried to turn back, it started to rain, and lighten and thunder in a very dreadful manner.

Where are we now? asked Hopeful without hope. His companion didn't answer. He was completely lost. For the deluge had caused the waters to rise amain, and wash away the path. They were even in great danger of being drowned, had they not found a narrow ledge with an overhanging rock. Here they sheltered, as best they could, and waited for the dawn. And being tired out, they fell asleep.

It was broad daylight when they were awakened by a grim and surly voice.

What are you doing, it said, *in my private grounds?*

Looking up, they saw before them the gloomy figure of Giant Despair, owner of Doubting Castle, out for his morning walk.

We're just poor pilgrims, who've lost our way, they said.

You're trespassing, said the Giant.

Trampling down my fields. I'll have to teach you a lesson.

They had little to say. They knew they were in the wrong, and since he was stronger than they, they were forced to accompany him. In the light of day, they could now see before them the battlements of Doubting Castle.

Here they were cast into a dungeon, dark and stinking. And here they lay from Wednesday morning till Saturday night, without one bite of bread or one drop of water. No one came to visit them. They were cut off from their friends; no one knew where they were. Christian realized it was all his fault for taking the short-cut, and this caused him double sorrow.

Now Giant Despair had a wife. Her name was Diffidence. He never did anything without consulting her, and she was even more malevolent than he was. So, when he was gone to bed, she asked him about the prisoners — who they were, whence they came, and whither they were bound. He told her, and asked her what he should do with them.

You're too soft-hearted, she said. *What you must do, when you get up in the morning, is to beat them without mercy!*

So, in the morning, he cut himself a grievous cudgel from a crab-apple tree in his garden. Then, railing upon his prisoners, as if they were dogs — though they had never uttered a word against him — he beat them most fearfully, and left them helpless on the floor, to spend another day in sighs and lamentations

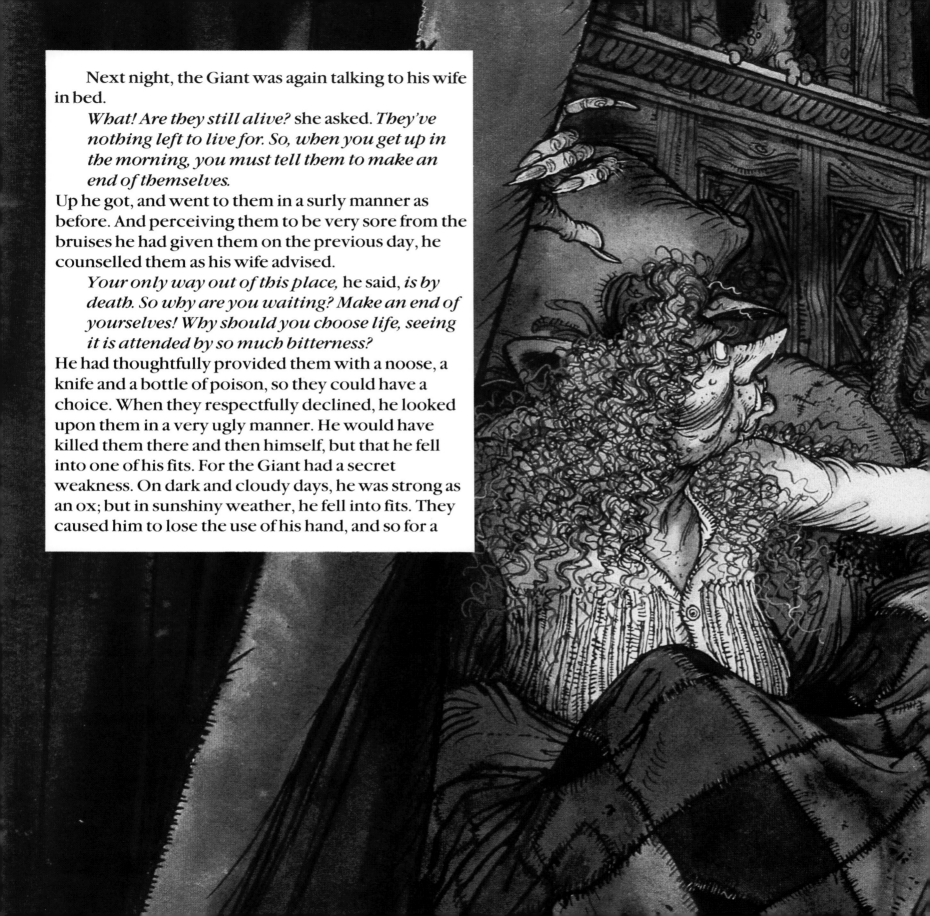

Next night, the Giant was again talking to his wife in bed.

What! Are they still alive? she asked. *They've nothing left to live for. So, when you get up in the morning, you must tell them to make an end of themselves.*

Up he got, and went to them in a surly manner as before. And perceiving them to be very sore from the bruises he had given them on the previous day, he counselled them as his wife advised.

Your only way out of this place, he said, *is by death. So why are you waiting? Make an end of yourselves! Why should you choose life, seeing it is attended by so much bitterness?*

He had thoughtfully provided them with a noose, a knife and a bottle of poison, so they could have a choice. When they respectfully declined, he looked upon them in a very ugly manner. He would have killed them there and then himself, but that he fell into one of his fits. For the Giant had a secret weakness. On dark and cloudy days, he was strong as an ox; but in sunshiny weather, he fell into fits. They caused him to lose the use of his hand, and so for a

time he had to withdraw. Then Christian and Hopeful discussed among themselves what they should do.

Perhaps the Giant is right, said Christian. *Perhaps death would be better than the miserable life we lead.*

Not everything is in the hands of the Giant Despair, said Hopeful. *Who knows but he may have another of his fits, and forget to lock us in. Let us not be our own murderers.*

In this way Hopeful moderated the mind of his brother. And so they continued together, another day in the dark.

Then, night being come, and the Giant and his wife being in bed, she asked him again about the prisoners. To which he replied:

They are sturdy rogues. They choose to bear all hardships rather than make away with themselves.

Then here's what you must do, she said. *Tomorrow morning take them to the castle-yard, and show them the bones and skulls of those whom you have already despatched.*

Up got the Giant once again, and took his prisoners into the castle-yard, as his wife had bidden him.

These, he said, pointing to the skeletons, *were pilgrims just like you, who trespassed in my grounds. When I thought fit, I tore them in pieces, as, within ten days, I will do to you.*

Back in their dungeon, Christian nearly swooned away. For now, through lack of food and by reason of his bruises, he could hardly breathe. But Hopeful again encouraged him.

My brother, he said, *Apollyon couldn't crush you, nor the Valley of the Shadow of Death. And remember how you played the man in Vanity Fair. Don't forget I'm in the dungeon with you, a far weaker man by nature than you are. This Giant has wounded me as well as you, and cut off the bread and water from my mouth. And, like you, I'm deprived of light. So let us exercise a little more patience, and bear up as best we can, and keep on praying.*

Then — as often happens in dreams, when things are desperate — Christian suddenly remembered.

I have in my pocket, he said, *an old key called Promise. It might just fit the lock.*

Try it, said Hopeful, hopefully.

It was the middle of the night when Diffidence sat up in bed and roused her husband.

Perhaps, she said, *they have pick-locks with them. That's why they live in hope.*

Sayest thou so, my dear, said Giant Despair. *I'll search them in the morning. That's time enough.*

Even then, Christian was trying the dungeon door with his key. The lock went damnable hard; weak as he was, he had to work at it. But at last the key began to turn. There was a creaking and groaning, and the door swung open, and in came the light of dawn.

What's that noise? said the Giant, waking with a start.

Better go and see, my dear, said his wife.

Christian and Hopeful had run through the door, only to be confronted by a new obstacle, a heavy iron gate.

Try the key again, said Hopeful.

Christian tried it, and it worked.

Then the Giant was upon them.

Nothing can save us now, cried Christian. *All is lost!*

But no sooner had the Giant come into the light of the sun, than he had another of his fits. His limbs failed him, and his legs gave way.

Christian and Hopeful were quickly out of the Castle Grounds, and out of the Giant's jurisdiction. At the place where they had gone astray, they now put up a notice:

OVER THIS STILE IS THE WAY TO DOUBTING CASTLE. ALL TRESPASSERS WILL BE DESTROYED. TAKE WARNING

That done, they continued in safety on the King's Highway. But not, I fear, for very long.

97

The Dark River

Christian, and his new friend Hopeful, had now reached the Delectable Mountains, which Christian had seen from the Palace Beautiful. And what a pleasant change was here! After the squalor of the Giant's prison, they were able to wash themselves in clear streams, and to eat freely the fruit of the orchards.

Next they were met by a party of shepherds, feeding their flocks, who led them most lovingly to a topmost peak.

From here, they said, *is your first glimpse of the Celestial City — if you have skill to look through our perspective glass.*

They looked, and thought they saw what might have been a Golden Gate.

I saw also in my dream that, as they stood leaning on their staffs — the way that weary pilgrims do — the shepherds gave them these two warnings:

1 *Beware of the Flatterer.*
2 *Take heed of the Enchanted Ground.*

With that, they sent them on their way.

Now, from a crooked lane ahead of them, appeared a brisk young lad; his name was Ignorance. He'd set out that morning from the Country of Conceit to walk to the Celestial City. Christian proceeded to question him:

But you didn't come in by the wicket-gate. You came in by this crooked lane.

I couldn't be expected to go all the way back, said Ignorance.

Then what have you to show at the Gate of Heaven? Christian asked. *Have you your parchment?*

Oh no, I shan't need that, said Ignorance.

But they may take you for a thief or a robber, warned Christian.

Gentlemen, you are utter strangers to me, said Ignorance. *Be content to practise your religion, and I will practise mine. I'm sure all will be well.*

He clearly wouldn't listen to advice. So they left the lad to follow on behind.

Arriving at a place where two ways met, they were wondering which way to go, when behold a man dressed in white came up to them. (They supposed he was one of the Shining Ones.) Hearing that they were bound for Heaven's Gate, he said to them most civilly:

I'm going there myself, so follow me.

But the road kept bending round and round, till presently they found themselves with the City quite behind them.

This can't be right, they said, and tried to stop.

But all too late! For they had got entangled in a net they hadn't seen, which was drawn across their path. The more they tried to free themselves, the more enmeshed did they become. As to the man in white, he'd thrown off his robe, and was revealed for what he was — a villainous being, who mockingly abandoned them. They might have languished there all day, had not a real Shining One appeared, and cut the net, and set them free.

Did no one warn you against the Flatterer? the Angel asked.

The Shepherds did, said Christian. *But we never thought that this fine-spoken man was he.*

They were back on their right road again, with
Ignorance still following behind, when yet another
traveller was seen coming to meet them. His name
was Atheist, and when he heard where they were
going he broke into loud laughter.

I laugh to see what ignorant persons you are,
explained Atheist, *to take so tedious a journey,
and then have nothing to show at the end of it.
Why, sir, do you think we shan't be received?
Received?* Atheist repeated. *There's no such
place. I've been looking for this City for twenty
years. Heaven does not exist.*
So saying, he swept past them on his way. But they
knew better, having lately seen the City through the
Shepherds' telescope.

And I saw then in my dream that, as they were passing through a certain vale, a gradual weariness assailed their limbs. The air was heavy, as before a storm; and they grew very drowsy.

I can hardly keep my eyes open, said Hopeful to his fellow. *Let's stop, and take a nap. For 'sleep is sweet to the labouring man', and we may wake refreshed.*

Equally, said Christian, *we may never wake again. For this, methinks, is the Enchanted Ground, of which the Shepherds warned us.*

Poor Hopeful looked aghast at being so unwise.

Had I been here alone, he said, *I must have met my death!*

For now, indeed it felt as if someone had cast a spell on them. But they were not to be ensnared a second time.

We'll keep ourselves awake by good discourse, said Christian, stifling a yawn.

And talking all the while, they forced their feet along, and so made their escape.

They entered now a country where the air was sweet again. The flowers grew, the birds all sang, and the sun shone night and day. For this was the land of Beulah, where the Shining Ones commonly walked; and it lay upon the frontier of Heaven.

Behind them, they could just see, looking back, a shadow in the sky, which marked the place where Doubting Castle stood. But ahead, there was a perfect view of the Celestial City, a City founded higher than the clouds. Its walls and towers shone in the sun, so dazzling that pilgrims had to look at it through clouded glass, until their eyes grew more accustomed to the light.

Then, just as they imagined they were safely there, they all at once stood still, quite stunned by what they saw. For, between them and the City Gate, flowed a deep, dark River, over which a mist for ever swirled. They looked to the left, and they looked to the right. But the men on the bank said:

You have to go through it. There is no bridge.

It was a fearful moment, for Christian couldn't swim. Yet, after coming all that way, he mustn't falter now. He stepped into the River trembling, and immediately began to sink. He shouted to his good friend:

Hopeful! Hopeful! The waves are swallowing me up!

Hopeful tried to keep his head above water. But the River was so deep that Christian sank again. He was more frightened now than he had ever been, even in the Valley of the Shadow. A great darkness and horror fell upon him. For this was the River of Death. And he feared he was drowning in it.

But the troubles a man goes through in these waters are no sign that God has forsaken him. All at once the sun was visible through the mist. The pilgrims felt new strength within themselves, the water became less deep, the ground was firmer underfoot. And so they reached the shore.

Meanwhile what of Ignorance, who was never far behind? He got over without half the difficulty of the others, and didn't even wet his shoes. For he had met a dubious ferryman, called Vain-hope, who ferried him across.

Upon the farther bank, two men in shining clothes were standing to receive our friends.

It's you, it's you they wait for, said Christian to Hopeful. *You have been Hopeful ever since I knew you.*

And so have you, said he to Christian.

Now you must note that the City stood upon mighty hill, but the pilgrims went up that hill with much agility and speed. They had such glorious companions to take them by the arm.

But no one was there to welcome Ignorance. He had to climb the path alone.

Then, as the pilgrims neared the Gate, the whole of the Heavenly Host must have known of their arrival. For they were greeted by the King's Own Trumpeters, who made all Heaven echo with their sound.

But when Ignorance knocked to be admitted, the men above the Gate looked down on him and said:

Where is your parchment-roll. my friend, to prove that you have come by the right road?
He fumbled in his coat, but having nothing—as we know—stood silent underneath their gaze, then sorrowfully turned back. That was the last we saw of Ignorance.

The pilgrims, on the other hand, both had their parchments ready, and a voice cried out:

These pilgrims now are come from the City of Destruction for the love they bear to the King of this place.
So the Gates of Heaven opened to them, and they entered in.

And, writes Bunyan in his book, *I was able to look in after them, I saw the streets were paved with gold. And in them walked—with crowns upon their heads—the company of just men made perfect. And the bells of the City rang for joy. For Christian and his fellow had come to their true home. And after that, they shut the Gates, and I awoke. And behold, it was a dream.*

9

Christiana's Story

I slept and dreamed again, of Christiana, Christian's wife. Behold she sat alone, remembering the brinish tears of her husband, and how she did harden her heart against all his entreaties to go with him to the Celestial City. And now she was regretting it; for she had lost her dearest friend, and the loving bond between them had been broken. She knew full well it was for the love that he had to his Prince that he ventured as he did.

While thus she mused, there came a knocking at the door.

If you come in God's name, enter, she said

It was a stranger who appeared before her.

My name, he said, *is Secret. I live with those on high. And I bring this letter to you from your husband's Prince.*

She opened it with trembling hands. It smelt of the best perfume, and was written in letters of gold. It was an invitation to do what Christian himself had done, to make that dangerous journey — both she and her four sons.

It was what she believed she ought to do. So as soon as her visitor had gone, she rose and packed her bags. Two of her neighbours, when they saw it, were quite stunned. One whose name was Timorous, said:

Oh the madness that's possessed you! If your husband, being a man, was so hard put to it, what can you, a poor woman, do?

But young Mercy (for she was but young) offered to go with Christiana. At which she did rejoice.

For the Prince, she said, *who has sent for me, is one that delights in Mercy.*

Presently, in good weather, they started out — two women and four boys — to find the wicket-gate. The boys, who were called Matthew, Samuel, Joseph and James, went on ahead.

The road led them past a Castle wall, and on the other side of the wall was a garden, and some of the fruit trees grew over the wall. So Christiana's boys, as boys are apt to do, did pluck the fruit and began to eat. Their mother chided them, but if she had known to whom the fruit belonged she would have been ready to die of fright. Even now, from beyond the wall, a hideous barking could be heard.

Why do they keep such a filthy cur? cried Mercy, much affrighted.

They ought to hang it, said the boys.

But everybody greatly feared that it would jump into the road, and do to them what its doggish nature prompted it to do.

114

They tried to hurry on, only to find their way was blocked by two ill-favoured men.

Stand back! the women cried, covering their faces with their shawls, and seeking to avoid a scuffle

We are in haste!

But the ruffians regarded not their words, and began to lay their brutal hands on them.

Murder! they shrieked. *Murder!*

Luckily, their cries were heard by the Keeper of the Gate — Goodwill, by name, as we recall — who hastened to the rescue; and the ruffians escaped over the wall.

That is Beelzebub's Castle, said their rescuer. *He is the owner of the dog, which has frightened many an honest pilgrim. And these men are his minions. But why did you not ask for a guide? Alas,* said Christiana, *who could have thought that, near your wicket-gate, there lurked such naughty ones.*

But a remedy was soon to hand. For, when they reached the House of the Interpreter, he summoned a Mr Great-heart, a manservant of his, and ordered him, from that day forth, to be their guardian, and guide them on their way.

Next morning they were off again, and shortly reached the place where Christian fought with the Foul Fiend, Apollyon.

Whereabouts was the battle — for the valley is large? asked one of the boys.

They fought in this narrow passage, said Mr Great-heart. *It's the most dangerous place in all these parts.* Then he called to Christiana: *Here are some of the shivers of Apollyon's darts. And here to this day upon these stones is some of your husband's blood — to prove how well he played the man.*

So they came to that evil haunted place, the Valley of the Shadow of Death. Many have spoken of it, but none can tell what the Valley is like, until they come to it themselves. And Mr Great-heart told of a Mr Fearing, who came on a pilgrimage with him once.

When we came to the entrance of this Valley, he said, *I thought I should have lost my man, he was so terrified. 'Oh the hobgoblins will have me! The hobgoblins will have me!' he cried.*

But they went through it better than Mr Fearing, and better far than Christian did, because they had the daylight, and Mr Great-heart was their guide. Even so, they heard a lot of groaning, as of dead men, which caused the boys to quake, and caused the women to look pale and wan.

Then a shadowy shape appeared, and Joseph cried:

Mother, What is it?

An ugly thing, child, she said. *An ugly thing, And now I see what your poor father has gone through. He went here all alone, by night and with these Foul Fiends busy all around him.*

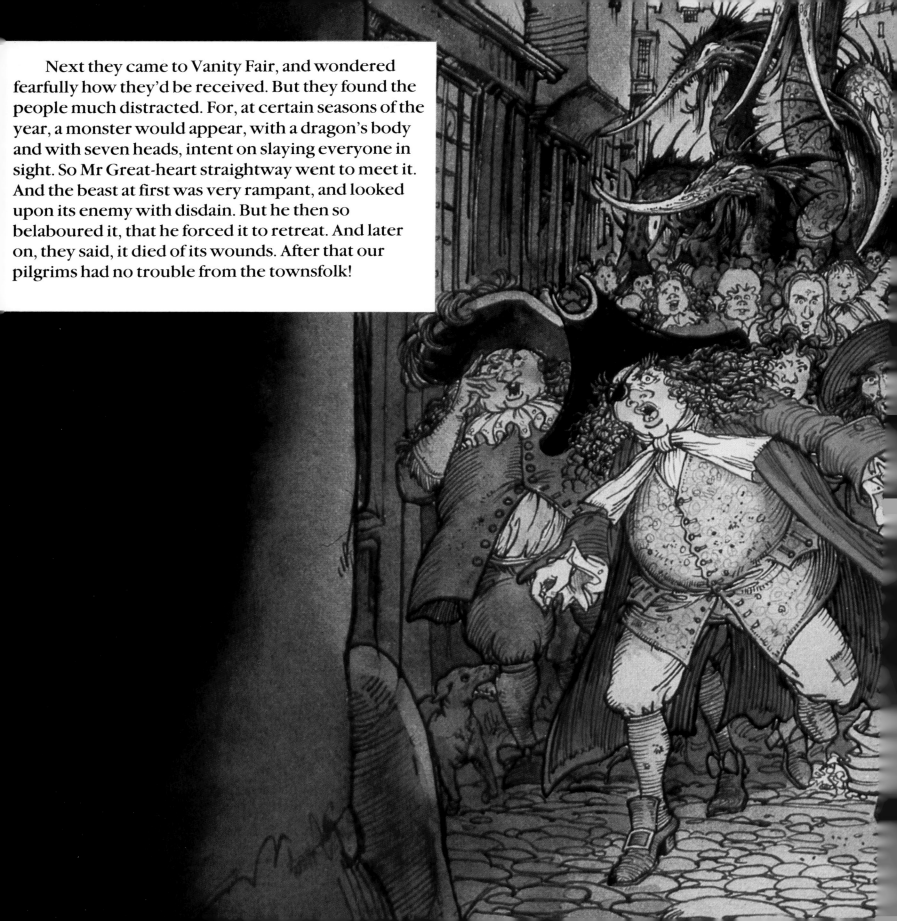

Next they came to Vanity Fair, and wondered fearfully how they'd be received. But they found the people much distracted. For, at certain seasons of the year, a monster would appear, with a dragon's body and with seven heads, intent on slaying everyone in sight. So Mr Great-heart straightway went to meet it. And the beast at first was very rampant, and looked upon its enemy with disdain. But he then so belaboured it, that he forced it to retreat. And later on, they said, it died of its wounds. After that our pilgrims had no trouble from the townsfolk!

Now as they went upon their way, they came to that same stile, which led to Doubting Castle. Here Mr Great-heart stopped to consider what must be done.

Have I not been commanded. he said, *to fight the good fight? And with whom should I fight, if not with Giant Despair. So who will go with me?*
We will! shouted Christiana's sons.

And though their mother would be anxious, still she let them go.

Now Giant Despair, because he was a giant, thought no one could overcome him. So, after receiving the challenge, he roared:

Who and what is this Mr Great-heart, that he thinks he can molest me — I who have made a conquest of Angels?

And he came out of his Castle, carrying a great club in his hand. But the boys beset him behind and before, like David of old, with slings and stones, and they brought him to the ground. The giant struggled hard, and was very loth to die. He had, as they say, as many lives as a cat. But Great-heart was his death, and severed the head from his shoulders. Diffidence, the giantess, was also cut down, and they buried them both under a heap of stones.

So they fell to demolishing Doubting Castle — a task which took them seven days. And there they found Mr Despondency, almost starved to death, and Much-afraid, his daughter. These two they saved alive. But you would marvel to have seen how full of dead men's bones the Castle was.

To celebrate their victory over so dangerous an enemy, Christiana played the viol and Mercy played the lute, and the boys all danced, and Mr Great-heart too. I promise you, they footed it well, and were jocund and merry. As to Mr Despondency, he was for feeding rather than dancing, so Christiana gave him food to eat. And in a while the old gentleman came to himself, and was revived.

As they continued on their way, there stood before them a man with his sword drawn, and his face all bloody. His name, he said, was Valiant-for-Truth, and he had lately been set upon by three villains and vanquished them.

Here are great odds: three against one, cried Great-heart.

It is true, replied Valiant-for-Truth, *but little or more are nothing to him that has the truth on his side.*

You have done well, said Great-heart.

Then they took him and washed his wounds. And Mr Great-heart was delighted in him; for he had found a man after his own heart, and because there were in his party them that were feeble and weak.

So they all went on together, now a company of ten: Mr Great-heart in lead, while Valiant-for-Truth was last in the line, in case some fiend or giant should attack them in the rear, and so do mischief. Now on all this road there wasn't a single inn, to refresh the feebler sort, and the way was deep in mud and slabbiness. Some of the children lost their shoes; and loud was the grunting, and the puffing, and the sighing.

To make things worse, night fell. But, prudently, their guide had brought a map, showing all the roads to the Celestial City. He now struck a light — for he never went without his tinder-box — and saw that they must make a right turn. Otherwise they might have all been sucked under in the mud, placed there on purpose by the Devil to destroy them.

So they arrived at Beulah, where there was an inn at last. And there came a post from the Celestial City, inquiring after Christiana, the wife of Christian the pilgrim. He had a summons from his Prince for her to appear before him within ten days. Now the River, which all pilgrims have to cross, had at that point its ebbings and its flowings. For some of it overflowed its banks; for others it was dry. So Christiana, having said farewell to all her family and friends, entered the water. To her relief it was quite shallow, and the last words she was heard to say were:

I come, O Lord, I come.
As to her children, says John Bunyan in his dream, *I didn't wait to see them cross. They stayed with Mercy and with Mr Great-heart, till their time was come.*

But a summons *had* arrived by the same post for Mr Valiant-for-Truth. Calling to his friends, he said:

My sword I give to him that shall succeed me, and my courage to him that can get it. My scars I carry with me as my witness that I have fought the Lord's battles.

As he entered the River, he said again:

Death, where is thy sting?

And as he went down deeper, he said:

Grave, where is thy victory?

So he passed over, and all the trumpets sounded for him on the other side.